EDWARD ('EDDIE') JOHN C
age when he wrote these stories i
junior school. He was a fun-lovin_
devoted brother to his younger sister, Amy.

Throughout his young life, Edward loved his sport and went on to play football and cricket at local, county and regional levels. In 1997, he graduated with a Sports Science degree from Loughborough University. After completing his PGCE in 1998, he began his teaching career at The Ridings High School in Bristol.

At twenty-four years old he was diagnosed with leukaemia. After four months of treatment he lost his battle with the disease.

Edward's creative writing exercise books were found twenty years later and his family felt that you would like to share in his 'Edventures'.

All proceeds from the book will go to the charity Blood Cancer UK.

EDVENTURES
of a Seven Year Old

Edward Gregg

SilverWood

Published in 2021 by SilverWood Books

SilverWood Books Ltd
14 Small Street, Bristol, BS1 1DE, United Kingdom
www.silverwoodbooks.co.uk

ISBN 978-1-80042-101-1

British Library Cataloguing in Publication Data
A CIP catalogue record for this book is
available from the British Library

Page design and typesetting by SilverWood Books

Dedicated to Amy, a devoted and beloved sister

Myself

My name is Edward. I am seven years old. I am quite tall and have blonde straight hair. My eyes are blue.

I live with my mummy and daddy and my sister Amy. She is one year old and has just started walking. My best toys are Subuteo and Test Match because they are my favourite sports. I love Captain Zep on the television because it lets you do it. I love chips to eat and the thing I like at school is reading.

My Grandad

My grandad's name is Charlie. He is very funny. For instance, we were at the golf course and my dad said to me, 'You are not playing as well as you usually do. Don't address the ball.'

My grandad said to the ball, 'Hello, ball. Nice day, isn't it?'

That is the sort of thing he does. He has grey hair and is retired. He comes to football every week. He has blue eyes and used to be an electrician. He gives me sweets and toffees.

Once a rake was in his path. He accidentally stepped on it and it came up and hit him on the nose. He had a big bruise on it!

Life as a Lamb

The first thing I ever saw was some men fussing over me. I was in this bag thing where there was not much air to breathe. My mother licked the bag off and I was glad, as then I had fresh air to breathe. My mother was standing up. I thought it was easy, so I tried but I couldn't do it. I just could not stand up. I kept flopping down. Again and again I tried, but I could not do it. I gave up in the end.

It's fun in the hills because you can run about with your friends. But, you have to be aware because sometimes the dog comes! That means it's time to be shorn. When you're being shorn, it tickles but you have to be careful as you might get cut. Shearing is always done by the farmer.

Dipping is also done by the farmer. The thing about dipping is that you change pens so many times that you lose count. When you finally get dipped the farmer ducks you under, when you come back up you are glad to see daylight!

A few months later you are taken to market to be sold.

Is There Anybody There?

'Is there anybody there?' I say as I knock on the door of an old house.

The house is very big. The door opens very slowly and it creaks.

'Hello? Can you…' Then suddenly I stop. There's no one there.

SLAM! The door shuts behind me. I quickly spin around and I see the key turning, but nobody is there to turn it!

I am getting really scared. I go up the stairs. Every one creaks. I go into a room and the wind blows the curtains. It makes my blood run cold.

When the wind dies down, the window shuts. This place must be haunted.

Footsteps are coming up the stairs. 'Oh, no, no, no…' I stammer. I must get out of the window. It's locked. I try the door. It's also locked! I hear a key turning in the keyhole.

The door flies open!

'HELP!' I shout. There is nobody there!

I run. I can hear footsteps behind me, growing louder and louder. The door ahead of me is open, but it is going to close! SLAM! I just got out. That was close!

A Sporting World

One day, I was at my nanny's house. I went upstairs to play with a box of toys my nan kept in the wardrobe. As I looked for them, I fell into the wardrobe. I was surprised that I did not hit my head on the back of the wardrobe. In fact, I wasn't even in the wardrobe, I was in another world.

A ball hit me on the head.

What kind of ball?

I soon knew because someone said, 'Fifteen, love'.

Then another voice, in an accent I didn't know (not Scottish), said, 'You cannot be serious man!'

I thought to myself, that is a famous tennis player.

I carried on and I heard a crash. It was something hitting a window. It was a cricket ball. I then heard something that sounded like a tweet, so I knew that a famous umpire with Bird for a surname was there. Then I heard cheering, it was a football match. I saw the whole game. The final score was City 5, Rovers 0.

The Man who Won and Lost the Pools

A man called Fred had just got home from work. He worked in a Yorkshire factory. He turned on the television to see the football results. He looked at it and this is how it read:

Sheffield 1	Liverpool 0
Watford 2	Stoke 0

'Drat!' he said and banged his fist on the table. Stoke lost again!

He went every Saturday to Stokes' ground, but he could not go to the away matches.

'Teatime,' shouted his wife.

'Aye, alright, Martha. What have we got?' said Fred.

'Fish and chips from the chippy,' said Martha.

'Have you got them?' asked Fred.

'No, you can get them,' she replied.

'Aye, I suppose so,' replied Fred.

After tea he checked his pools coupon. It said a possible jackpot! You should have seen the grin on Fred's face. 'Hey,

Martha. I've won the pools!' said Fred.

'You're pulling me leg!' said Martha.

'How can I pull your leg? You're in the other room!' said Fred. 'I'll claim it tomorrow. I am going to celebrate by going out with some mates, to the pub.'

Fred came home at one o'clock the next morning. He went to bed, then got up at nine o'clock to collect his winnings. On his way, he met two brothers, Jack and Jim, who were walking down the high street. Jim said, 'Fancy you winning the pools,' and he gave Fred a push. The coupon went flying out of Fred's hand and down the drain. Broken-hearted Fred went home. He couldn't sleep at all and in the morning he didn't go to work.

He went to work the next day, but something strange happened. His wife was washing up when a football coupon came out of the tap! As soon as Fred heard the news, he rushed out to claim his fortune, as it had to be that day!

The man at the pools said, 'Why is this late?'

Fred answered, 'It is a long story.'

The Great Escape

It was my court trial. I was in the dock, hearing the magistrate read out my punishment. It really was the worst possible punishment. A shiver went down my spine when he finished. I was to go and receive my punishment right that minute.

I went into a dark room. They were not being kind to me as there was no food or water. Suddenly a panel slipped beneath my feet! I jumped out of the way and just managed to jump into a cage. Suddenly, the bars of the cage were set alight. There was fire all around me, getting closer and closer. There was heat all around me. I pushed my back against the bars, but they only scorched and burnt me.

I thought this would be my fate, to be burnt, but then spikes came out and I grabbed one of them. It was too hot. I saw there was a hole where I stood, so eventually I let go and fell down the hole.

There was a monster there!

I had an idea: I got in front of a rock. The monster ran

at me…I dodged…he broke the rock and died because he hit a sharp piece.

'I am free,' I thought.

I emigrated to another country and nobody knew that I had escaped from the 'Valley of Death'.

Fox Cubs

Two little fox cubs peep through the grass that surrounds their den. They look shy. Suddenly their ears prick up as they hear something coming. They quickly dart into their den. They come out when the coast is clear and have a play fight.

I think their fur is like a ginger biscuit. Their black, beady eyes watch every movement. If they see something they would like to eat, they swiftly run towards it. Sometimes the animal gets away but most of the time they catch it. The catch becomes a tasty morsel for the fox to chew on.

Some people think that the fox is the cleverest animal in the world. I will tell you something, they may be right.

Mary and Martin in the Shed

Mary and Martin are busy in the shed. Martin is making a pot for Mother's Day. He is hammering a nail into a piece of wood.

Mary says, 'Look, Martin, I have found the right size piece of wood.'

Martin looks up and brings his hammer down at the same time, missing the nail and breaking the wood he was working on. 'Now look what you made me do!' says Martin.

So he gets another piece of wood. Everything is alright until he starts doing heavy strokes. His grip is not very firm and as he pulls his arm back, the hammer goes flying out of his hand and hits the window. SMASH!

'Oh no!' says Mary.

There's still one more tragedy. All went well until they decide they need some paint. Martin can't find the paint. He turns around, hits a shelf and gets a paint pot on his head. Eventually, they get the pot finished.

Their mum is pleased and says, 'It must have been easy!'

My Kite

I got a kite for Christmas. I came downstairs one morning and a gale was blowing. I said to my dad, 'This is a good day for flying my kite.'

My dad said, 'Not yet, wait until the wind has calmed down a bit or it will blow you away.'

This made me laugh.

After breakfast the wind had calmed down and so I went into the garage to get my new kite. My mum called, 'Where are you going?'

'I am going to fly my kite up on the common,' I said.

'Don't you think your dad should come with you?' said Mum.

'I'll be okay by myself. The common is not far away,' I said.

So off I went to fly my kite. When I got to the common, other people were flying kites. Then I wanted to fly my kite. My kite was rectangular in shape and blue and red in colour. I unwound the ball of string and it went high in the trees.

But I didn't spot some very tall trees and the kite got stuck on the top branch!

I couldn't climb the tree and it was nearly dinner time. 'Oh dear,' I said to myself. Then, a sudden gust of wind blew and down came the kite…and off I went happy again.

The Day Dennis
Dropped the Eggs

One day Dennis went to his granny's house. It was a long way because Dennis lived in the town and his granny had a farm in the country. Never before had Dennis been on a farm and he was excited. He said to himself, 'I will be very helpful to Granny and Grandfather. I will feed the animals.'

Mummy had said not to chase any of the animals.

When they got there it was night-time. Dennis went into the front room where his granny was knitting and his grandfather was watching *Match of the Day*.

The next morning Dennis went to fetch the eggs from the hen house, but disaster struck. He forgot to take a basket. As he came out he dropped all the eggs.

His granny came out and said, 'What a naughty boy you are, Dennis.'

He never collected the eggs again!

The Black Box

The Black Box made a terrible buzzing sound. Then, a crackling sound came from inside the box. The children took off the lid of the box and there lay an egg. Then, out of the top of the egg jumped a Fuzz Buzz.

The Fuzz Buzz went a long way before he came upon a forest. Then he went a little way, before he came across a cave. He ventured inside and heard some sort of animal coming towards him!

So quickly he set a trap by digging a hole and putting a net over it. He filled the net with stones and a lot of meat.

He hid behind a rock and waited for the animal to come. The Fuzz Buzz could clearly see they were lions. When they saw the meat, they ran towards it. They jumped and grabbed the meat and then saw the Fuzz Buzz. The leader of the lions said, 'Look at that hairy thing over there.'

Very quickly, the Fuzz Buzz ran away and never went in the forest again!

Journey into Space

This was the day! This was the day I was going to go into space with Lee, my friend.

I thought I was dreaming when they asked me to go into space! 'Just think, the first boy in space,' I said.

I was going to America on a plane, which was my first flight alone, on the space shuttle Horizon.

When the time came for us to go on the plane, I said, 'Well, here we go!' It was such a tense moment for both of us when the plane took off. I said again, 'Here we go.'

Lee said, 'How many more times are you going to say, "Here we go!"?'

We both burst out laughing.

When we got to Kennedy Space Centre, they said we were going to lift off from there and land at Cape Canaveral. We got into the shuttle and listened to the countdown: 10...9...8...7...6...5...4...3...2...1. We pressed the red button and heard the voice again, this time he said, 'LIFT OFF!' It was amazing.

I said to Lee, 'I've flown a shuttle on a computer!'

Lee laughed.

Then we saw a satellite. It was white.

Soon we heard Mission Control saying, 'You are going to be weightless.'

'This will be fun,' I said to Lee.

It was fun, we did some somersaults.

I said, 'Our gymnastics' teacher will be pleased!'

'Why?' said Lee.

'Because I have just passed a gymnastic award!' I said.

'This is Mission Control to shuttle, do you read me?' we heard.

'We read you,' we said.

'You are going to land on Saturn,' we heard.

We landed on Saturn. I tell you, we were sweating. We landed with a BANG! We got our spacesuits on and walked onto Saturn. We collected some moon dust and had some fun.

After collecting the dust we said, 'Who can jump the highest?' We both jumped the same.

When we got back into the shuttle we took off and sailed through space like birds in the sky. We landed back on Earth smoothly. We stepped out and all the reporters were all around us.

We could truly say that it was the best experience of our lives.

My Adventures as a Mouse

When I was a mouse, I went on an adventure. I was a house mouse. I lived in a hole in the skirting board. I set out of my hole and I saw two goal nets together. I walked on them and I heard something chasing me! I turned around – a huge paw was just about to squash me. I dodged it. I'd heard of cat and mouse, but this was ridiculous. I raced away and thought, 'If I go under something small, he'll get stuck.'

So I raced under the fridge. He couldn't get under but now I had other problems as there was a spider there! The cat and the spider weren't the only ones there. Lucky for me, there was a dog there as well. He was in a bad mood and he chased the cat out of the house.

So I got out from under the fridge and the spider chased me. Then suddenly I heard heavy footsteps. 'It's not that cat again,' I said to myself. But it wasn't the cat as the footsteps were much louder. They were getting closer and closer.

Suddenly 'SQUASH'.

I would not like to say this, but the person (for that is what it was) had squashed the spider!

I thought I had better run quickly. The person could have squashed me, if I hadn't been so nimble on my feet. I went behind the sofa. Then I saw a mousetrap. I wondered what to do. Then I saw the cat again, it was waiting for me.

I had a brainwave. If I got the other side of the trap, I could pull it out. As I did so it snapped the bar and hit the wood. The cat thought I was dead so he went away. I escaped to my hole and breathed a sigh of relief.

'That was a great adventure,' I said to myself.

How the Giraffe got His Long Neck

Many years ago, giraffes did not have long necks. There was a giraffe called John. He decided to seek his fortune. He was in Russia when he met a man called Evil Abdailler. It was one of Evil's bad days as he got out of bed on the wrong side. He also banged his head. 'Where do you come from?' Evil said.

'Ah, pardon?' said John.

Evil asked John again and John said again, 'Pardon?'

'Is that all you can say, pardon? If people say pardon to you from now on your neck will grow an inch,' said Evil.

Quickly, John ran away and came to the King and Queen's palace. John told the King his story and they asked John to stay for tea.

In the middle of tea the King burped and the Queen said, 'I grant you a royal pardon. Oh, pardon me,' said the Queen.

John asked if he could leave as he didn't want his neck to grown any longer.

John went on and on to India. John was amazed by the tall buildings and so he did not see an Indian man running into his path. The man bumped into John and the worst thing happened.

The Indian man said, 'Oh golly gosh, a thousand pardons.'

So that is why giraffes have long necks.

Twenty-Six Miles and Eighty-Seven Yards

On a damp April morning, the sun was blazing through the trees and the puddles were reflecting a figure of a person jogging. It was me, training for a marathon. I had been training for months and there were two days to go. I needed some new trainers, so my mum bought me some that were supposed to be good. I relaxed the next day. Then, when the big day came, I got there early because I wanted to win. I needed a front position and had to wait half an hour before the race started.

BANG! Off went the gun and off we went too.

Everybody was cheering and clapping us as we jogged along the road. Already I was feeling tired. After five miles I saw what I needed, a drink. I was so thirsty I took two.

'Only twenty-one miles to go,' someone said.

'Thanks very much,' I said.

Two hours later it really hurt. I was on my last mile… and then I was on the finishing line. I collapsed.

I remember that damp April morning when everybody crowded around me.

A Day in the Life of My Teeth

It is very hot in a mouth at night so I am glad when morning comes and the person I belong to yawns and I get a breath of fresh air. When it is time to eat every tooth gets excited. And when the foods comes in everybody tries to get at it. When you cannot get at the food any more we shout, 'Coming down,' and away it goes.

Once the breakfast is over, it is time for a good wash. Now this is strange, because this thing comes into the mouth and scrubs you. After then it is off to school.

When it is cold some of us start chattering. When we are in school there is a lot of hard work to be done.

When school is over there is sometimes a trip to the dentist. Here the person I belong to always goes first. When he opens his mouth these shiny metal things come in. Then it is home to have some tea, watch TV, a brush again and off to bed.

The Red Indian*

It was my eighth birthday. When I went downstairs and opened a parcel, inside was an Indian outfit. It had a head-dress and a tunic. I was very keen to try it on, so changed and ran outside to have a good game.

I wanted to build a wigwam, so went to the garage to get some bean canes to build the wigwam frame. I asked my Mother for an old tablecloth to cover the frame. When I had done this I said to my Mum that I was hungry so I was going to make a bow and arrow to catch buffalo. And I did!

* n.b. we acknowledge Red Indian as an archaic and potentially offensive term, written by the author as a child.

Theodora the Witch

Theodora was a very wicked witch who lived in a dark, scary cave that was in a steep mountain where children played. But the trouble was Theodora did not like children. She absolutely hated them!

One night, a group of children came up the mountain and started to play.

Theodora said, 'I have an idea'

Because Theodora was a name that nobody had, she said to the children, 'If you can guess my name within three days you can play here anytime.'

Well, the children tried but they could not guess it. But on the third day, in the morning a boy called John heard Theodora singing this rhyme:

'Today I bake, tomorrow I brew, the next day I have all the mountain. How glad am I that no one knew it is Theodora I am named!'

John ran back and told the others and they had all of the mountain to themselves!

Storm at Sea

Some people do not know what it is like to be shipwrecked, but the people who sailed on the *Queen Harriet* do. I was one of those people. We were sailing to France and I was just finishing writing a postcard to my mum and dad. I heard a rumbling sound which sounded like thunder! Ah, I thought, that is only thunder. You get that sometimes. But when I went back to bed, I could not help wondering about it.

Next morning, I woke up before my friends (Simon, Justin and Ben). I decided to go for a walk on the deck. I came back sooner than I wanted to! 'Boys,' I cried, 'we are going to be shipwrecked.'

'Stop pulling our legs,' they said together.

'I think I have jetlag,' said Justin.

'You cannot get jetlag on a boat,' I said.

'Well…' Justin did not finish that sentence because a wave came crashing on the roof of our room. It made a tremendous noise.

We yelled, 'Let's get out of here!'

The noise was incredible.

'HELP!' we cried.

The storm died down and we knew it was coming close. There was no time to lose. The sea was still rough and the ship ran aground on an island. We all jumped off, glad to be free.

'That was some pleasure cruise,' said Simon.

'It was a pleasure cruise if you like nightmares,' I said.

We all laughed and luckily we didn't have a storm on the way back!

Blood Cancer UK

All proceeds from this book will go to the charity Blood Cancer UK. They fund research to take us closer to a cure and have already helped transform treatments. The charity is also there for people when they need someone to talk to, whether on the phone or online, and they offer health information people can trust. Find out more and donate at bloodcancer.org.uk

Lightning Source UK Ltd.
Milton Keynes UK
UKHW051147180921
390773UK00001B/7

* 9 7 8 1 8 0 0 4 2 1 0 1 1 *